This **ELMER** book belongs to:

. . . .

**In Memory of Barbara —
with love and thanks for Chantel, Chuck and Brett**

This paperback edition first published in 2009 by Andersen Press Ltd.
First published in Great Britain in 1997 by Andersen Press Ltd.,
20 Vauxhall Bridge Road, London SW1V 2SA.
Published in Australia by Random House Australia Pty.,
Level 3, 100 Pacific Highway, North Sydney, NSW 2060.
Copyright © David McKee, 1997.
The rights of David McKee to be identified as the author and illustrator
of this work have been asserted by him in accordance with the
Copyright, Designs and Patents Act, 1988.
All rights reserved.
Colour separated in Switzerland by Photolitho AG, Zürich.
Printed and bound in China.

10   9   8   7   6   5   4   3

British Library Cataloguing in Publication Data available.

ISBN 978 1 84939 136 8 (Book People edition)
ISBN 978 1 84270 773 9 (Trade paperback edition)
ISBN 978 1 84270 784 5 (paperback and CD edition)

This book has been printed on acid-free paper

ELMER
and the Wind

David McKee

Andersen Press

It was a very, very windy day. Elmer, the
patchwork elephant, was sheltering in a cave
with his elephant friends, some birds and cousin
Wilbur, who was playing tricks with his voice.
The elephants laughed when Wilbur made his
voice come from a hole at the back of
the cave.

"It's not a good day for flying," said a bird.
"It's a good day to be a heavy elephant," chuckled Elmer.
"An elephant can't be blown away."
"I bet even you are afraid to go out in this wind, Elmer," said the bird.
"Afraid?" said Elmer. "Watch this then. Come on, Wilbur."
"Come back, don't be silly," called the elephants.
But Elmer and Wilbur had already gone out into the wind.

Once they
were behind some
trees and out of sight
of the others, Elmer led the
way into another cave.
"You're up to something, Elmer," said Wilbur.
"Yes," laughed Elmer. "Make your voice come
from out there as if we were still walking away.
Sound like me sometimes."

"I get it," said Wilbur. His voice
came from the distance, sounding like Elmer –
"It's hard to move in this wind." Then like
himself – "Careful, Elmer, hold on."

The elephants heard the voices and started to worry.
Wilbur called, "Hold on to something, Elmer. Look out!"

"HELP!" came Elmer's voice. "HELP! I'm flying."
Wilbur called, "ELMER! COME BACK! ELMER! OH,
HELP! HELP!"

"Elmer's being blown away, we must help," said an elephant.

"If you go out you'll be blown away too," said a bird.

"Form a chain, trunks holding tails," said another elephant.

They crept out of the cave, each elephant holding the tail of the elephant in front.

"Look at them," said Elmer. "They do look funny."

"Come back, you'll be blown away," called Wilbur. The elephants all started to speak at once, but because they were holding on with their trunks, their voices sounded very strange:

"We've been fooled!"

"The rotters . . ."

"It's an Elmer and Wilbur trick."

Then they backed back into the cave and looked funnier than ever.

When they were safely back in the cave, Elmer and
Wilbur returned as well. The elephants enjoyed the joke
but a bird said, "That was very silly, Elmer."
"But really, Bird," said Elmer, "an elephant can't be
blown away. I'll walk to those trees and back to prove it."
"Another trick," said an elephant, as Elmer walked away.

They watched as Elmer disappeared behind
some trees.

Then they heard Elmer's voice calling, "Help! I can't
keep on the ground."

The elephants laughed, "Very funny, Wilbur."

The voice came again, "HELP! I'M FLYING!"

The elephants laughed louder than ever.

"It's not me this time," said Wilbur.

"Look!" said a bird. "It isn't Wilbur."
The elephants stared: there was Elmer above the trees.
"What's he doing up there?" gasped an elephant.
"It's called flying," said a bird.
"Poor Elmer," said an elephant.

"It's my ears," thought Elmer. "They're acting as wings."
Wilbur and the others seemed very small as he flew away.

"This is really quite fun," thought Elmer after a while. He could see the other animals sheltering from the wind. They stared to see an elephant fly by. "It's Elmer," said a lion. "I expect he's up to another of his tricks."

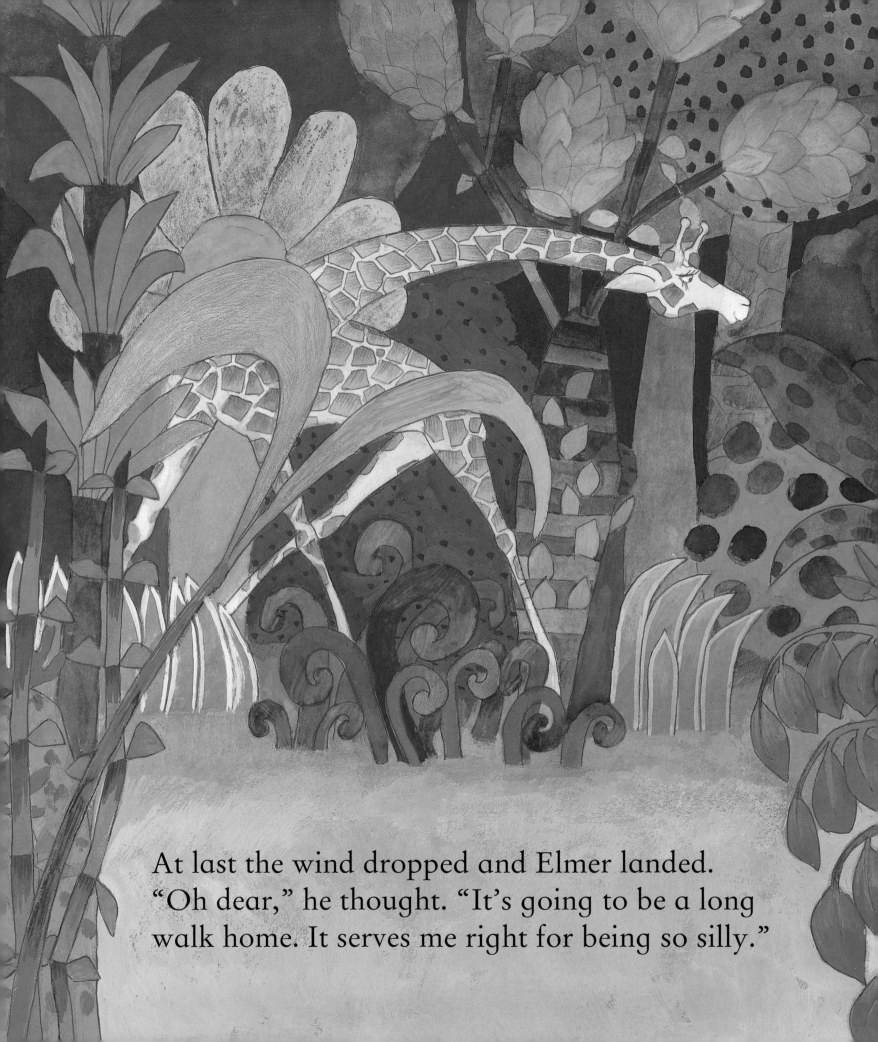

At last the wind dropped and Elmer landed.
"Oh dear," he thought. "It's going to be a long
walk home. It serves me right for being so silly."

When the wind stopped, the birds flew off to find Elmer and help guide him home. When at last the elephants saw the birds flying above the trees, they knew that Elmer was near. They rushed to meet him to hear about his adventure.

"You were wrong, Elmer," said the bird.
"An elephant can be blown away."
"You were wrong too, bird," laughed Elmer.
"It was a lovely day for flying!"

Read more ELMER stories

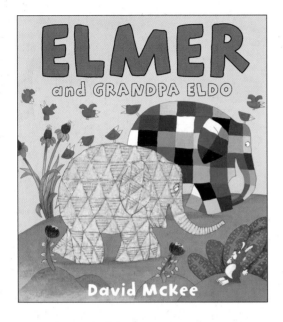

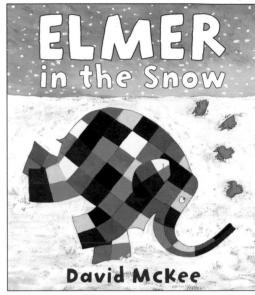

Also available as a book and CD

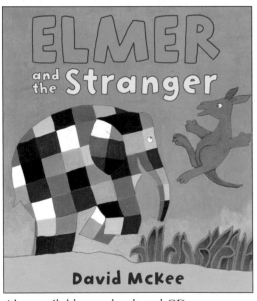

Also available as a book and CD

Also available as a book and CD

Find out more about David McKee and Elmer, visit:
www.andersenpress.co.uk/elmer

We Are Family

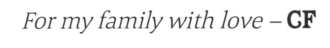

For my family with love – **CF**

To my big family with love – **JA**

SIMON & SCHUSTER

First published in Great Britain in 2018 by Simon & Schuster UK Ltd
1st Floor, 222 Gray's Inn Road, London WC1X 8HB
A CBS Company

Text copyright © 2018 Claire Freedman
Illustrations copyright © 2018 Giuditta Gaviraghi

ISBN: 978-1-4711-1716-9 (PB) • ISBN: 978-1-4711-7210-6 (eBook)
Printed in China • 10 9 8 7 6 5 4 3 2 1

We Are Family

Claire Freedman & Judi Abbot

SIMON & SCHUSTER

London   New York   Sydney   Toronto   New Delhi

Brothers and sisters are the **BEST!**
They make my life great fun.

Just sharing, caring, being there,
that's why I **LOVE** each one.

We make each other giggle
with the silly things we do,
like dressing up all scary,
jumping out and shouting . . .

We love it at the swimming pool,
and get there in a flash.
We all hold hands
and jump straight in
to make a giant . . .

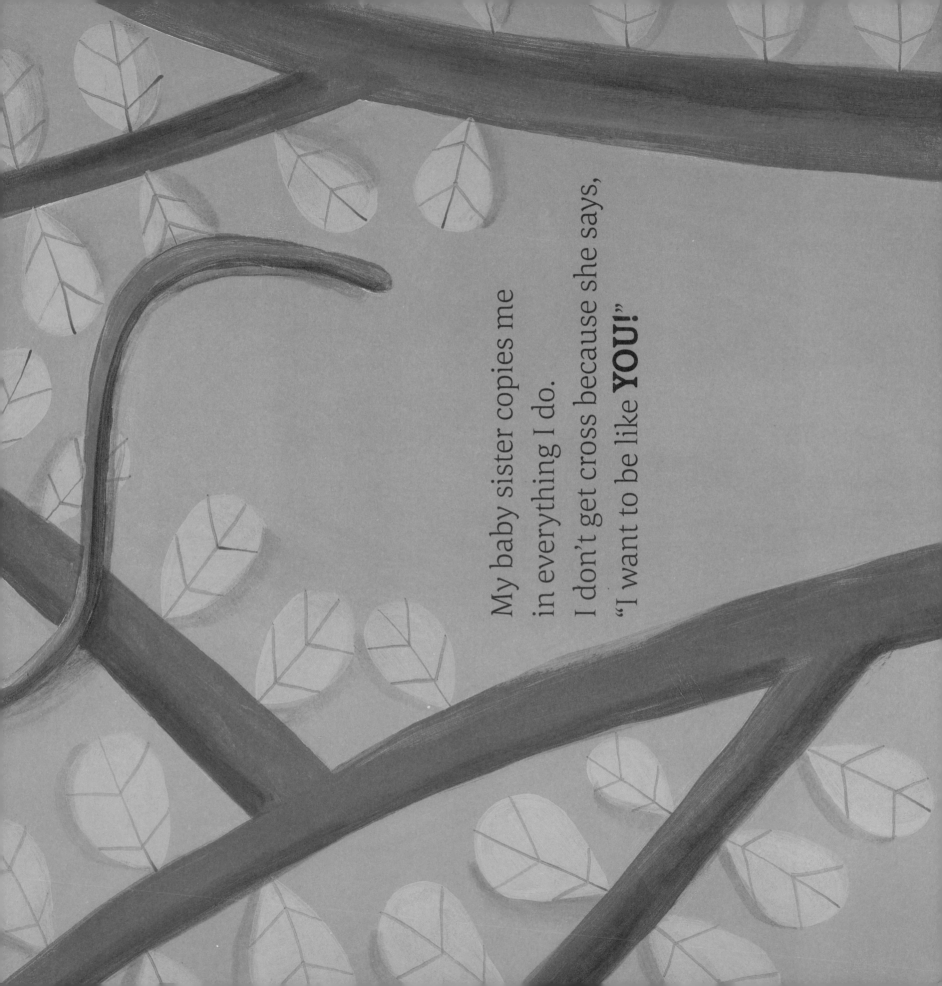

My baby sister copies me
in everything I do.
I don't get cross because she says,
"I want to be like **YOU!**"

When Mum buys yummy milkshakes,
which everyone enjoys,
the winner is the one who makes
the loudest **slurping** noise!

If one of us is feeling sad
we **rush** to find each other.
There's no one that can cuddle
like a sister or a brother.

Sometimes we fight and squabble,
but the quarrels **never** last.

Because we're closer than best friends
we make up **really** fast!

When Dad calls out,
"Who ate my cake?"
we **know** it was my brother ...

... but we pretend he's innocent
and stick up for each other!

My sister borrows all my things –
it's **really** hard to share.
But swapping toys can be great fun,
I love her teddy bear!

It's fun to teach my brother things,
I show him how to cook,

and help him say the **tricky** words
when he reads his new book.

We all put on a super show
(we practise hard all day),
then Mum and Dad sit down to watch
and clap and cheer . . .

Brothers and sisters are the **best**
and all of us agree,
through good days, bad days,
rain or shine,

we **LOVE** our family!